THE TRANSFORMERS
Robots
in Disguise!

They came from Cybertron—a planet of machines—where war raged for thousands of years between the noble Autobots and the evil Decepticons.

NOW THE BATTLE OF THESE POWERFUL ROBOTS IS YOUR BATTLE!

ONLY YOU can protect the earth from the evil destruction of the Decepticons!

Read the directions at the bottom of each page. Then decide what the Autobots should do next.

If you decide correctly, the Autobots will triumph! If you make the wrong choices, the unspeakable evil of the Decepticons will rule the world!

Hurry! The adventure begins on page 1.

THE TRANSFORMERS™

Decepticon Poison

by Judith Bauer Stamper

59093

BALLANTINE BOOKS · NEW YORK

Library of Congress Catalog Card Number: 85-91169

ISBN: 0-345-33073-0

Editorial Services by Parachute Press, Inc.

Illustrated by William Schmidt

Designed by Gene Siegel

Manufactured in the United States of America

First Edition: April 1986

10 9 8 7 6 5 4 3 2 1

THE TRANSFORMERS™

Decepticon Poison

Inside Autobot headquarters, engines are revving. A new fuel supply has just arrived. With their gas gauges reading near empty, the Autobots get ready to fuel up.

Sunstreaker zooms up to the silver tank first.

"Fill me up," he orders, his gleaming body screeching to a stop.

Sparkplug, the Autobots' human friend, grins at the stylish race car.

"Okay, hotshot," he says, and gives Sunstreaker a full tank.

Bluestreak, Cliffjumper, Brawn, and Warpath are next. Sparkplug pumps them full of fuel. Soon half the Autobots at headquarters are ready to roll.

A rumble goes through the room as mighty Optimus Prime shifts his tractor-trailer into gear. He pulls up to the tank with a big appetite.

Just then Red Alert rushes in. The Autobot security director's lights are flashing!

. . . .
Turn to page 2.

"Trouble," he roars. "Ramjet's been here. I just saw him flying west from headquarters. I wonder what that sneaky Decepticon was up to!"

"Transform! Right away," Optimus Prime orders his comrades. "And report to your command posts."

As usual, Sunstreaker wants to be first. He strains to turn into a robot. But he's stuck! The other Autobots who just refueled are having trouble too. Autobot headquarters is filled with groans, screeches, and creaks.

"Ugghh! I can't move," Sunstreaker moans.

Optimus Prime has changed into his robot form. He looks around at his fellow Autobots. Only those who didn't refuel have transformed.

"Our transforming powers are gone!" Cliff-jumper groans.

"We've been sabotaged!" Warpath sputters.

"It's the fuel!" Optimus Prime roars. He points an accusing finger at the fuel tank. "Something foul is in that fuel!"

"Ramjet," Mirage mutters angrily. "He was here on a sabotage mission. He poisoned the fuel!"

"We must act fast," Optimus Prime declares. "The Decepticons may return in full force at any time!"

Turn to page 8.

The cave is dark and dank. The four Autobots hide behind acid-pocked boulders along the walls.

"Only a Decepticon could live here," Bumblebee says with a shudder. "There's green slime everywhere."

"Look at those rats!" Prowl exclaims.

He points to rodents as big as cats. Their eyes are a fiery red and their fur glows neon green as they scuttle across the floor.

"They're mutants," Mirage says. "Breathing this filthy air has turned them into monsters!"

Optimus Prime motions his comrades forward into the depths of the cave. Finally they arrive at the Poison Lab. Beakers of evil-smelling chemicals bubble over blue flames. Bumblebee spies the one that they need—Autobot Poison Antidote!

Just then Decepticon voices echo from the rear of the cave.

"We've got to act fast!" Prowl warns.

"Mirage, this is a job for you," their leader decides. "You must steal that beaker of antidote . . . right from under their ugly noses!"

. . . .

Turn to page 61.

Mirage readies his rocket-dart rifle. Prowl loads his acid-pellet gun. Optimus Prime selects weapons from his artillery deck.

Then, at their leader's command, the Autobots destroy the Decepticon Poison Lab. The beakers of poison shatter, and the foul chemicals hiss onto the cave floor.

"Now, back to headquarters," Optimus Prime says.

He lifts the beaker of antidote in front of Ramjet and Starscream's eyes.

"Your plot against the humans has been foiled," he tells them. "And the Autobots will soon be back to full fighting power. We will never give up in our battle against Decepticon evil!"

But that's another story for another day . . . for the battle between the noble Autobots and the evil Decepticons can never really come to

THE END

"Remember our comrades at headquarters," Optimus Prime says. "They need this antidote. We must hurry back to save them."

"Good thinking," Bumblebee says. "Let's get out of here!"

The four Autobots move stealthily along the sides of the cave. Ramjet and Starscream are still plotting their evil deed on the opposite side of the lab.

"Ow!" Mirage mutters as his broad shoulders chip off a piece of sharp rock from the wall. The stone hits the floor with a loud thud.

"Get down!" Optimus Prime orders, crouching in a dark recess.

"What was that?" Ramjet's voice booms through the cave.

Just then one of the large mutant rats scuttles past Bumblebee. The little Autobot smothers his cry of surprise.

The rat runs into the view of the curious Decepticons.

"I thought I smelled a rat!" Starscream says, cackling and kicking the rat with one enormous foot.

Turn to page 20.

"We know the route to the Poison Lab," Mirage points out. "We could be back there within two hours."

Optimus Prime agrees. "We'll attempt to stop their poisonous plot before it starts!"

A short time later, a long caravan of Autobot vehicles winds toward the Decepticon hideout.

"How much farther?" Sunstreaker asks Bumblebee.

"You'll know when we're close," the mini-car answers. "Your carburetor will start choking. Your fan will clog up. And your exhaust system will work overtime!"

Finally the Autobots reach the top of the mountain above the lab.

"Quiet!" Optimus Prime commands. "We want a sneak attack!"

The Autobots shut off their engines. Slowly they coast down the hill. Suddenly their leader transforms and raises a mighty arm.

Then he points to the entrance of the Poison Lab.

"Wow!" Bumblebee murmurs.

Turn to page 40.

From a quiet corner of headquarters, Perceptor, the Autobot scientist, steps forward.

"This is a case of bad chemicals," he says. "Give me a sample of the fuel. I'll analyze it in my lab and formulate an antidote. Meanwhile, those of you who are healthy can guard headquarters against a Decepticon attack."

Optimus Prime begins to nod his head in agreement. Then Prowl steps forward.

"Your experiment may work, Perceptor," he declares, "but it may not. We can't wait around while you play with your chemistry set! A select group of us must pursue Ramjet. We'll use the small store of emergency fuel we keep. We must find the secret of the Decepticon poison and bring back a cure!"

Both strategies have their risks . . . and rewards! Perceptor's antidote could save the gasping Autobots . . . if it works . . . and if it's in time! Prowl's mission could reveal the Decepticons' entire plan . . . if it succeeds . . . and if they have sufficient firepower!

You must decide which path the Autobots will take!

. . . .
If you choose to let Perceptor try to find an antidote, turn to page 16.

If you choose Prowl's strategy for a fast attack, turn to page 24.

"I'm the military strategist," Prowl insists. "Let me take care of those poisons!

"Take cover behind that big boulder," he directs the other Autobots. "I'll fire my incendiary missiles from back here. The heat of the explosion will travel in the direction of Ramjet and Starscream. They'll lose their cool and collapse. The poisons will blow sky-high. Then we'll make our escape."

"He thinks," Bumblebee mutters under his breath.

The Autobots take their positions. Prowl aims his missiles at the poisons.

He fires!

Turn to page 48.

Everything below is scorched and polluted. Pine trees stand like bare, black skeletons. A stream runs with sluggish orange water. Yellow smog blots out the sunlight.

"The Decepticons!" Mirage guesses. "Who else could turn nature into this putrid mess?"

"Cut your engines," Optimus Prime orders. "We'll roll down the hill to check it out."

The Autobots begin the steep descent. Bumblebee worries about his brakes. He hopes Sparkplug fixed them during his last tune-up!

Soon the vehicles reach the valley floor. They take cover behind two towering redwoods. On the other side of the polluted stream they see the entrance to a cave. Yellow smoke curls from cracks at the top. A purple Decepticon symbol is painted above the entrance.

"That's what we're looking for," Prowl exclaims. "It must be the Decepticon Poison Lab!"

Turn to page 32.

"We must act now," Optimus Prime announces, "before it's too late!" He looks at his three comrades for agreement.

Bumblebee hesitates. He wants to get out of the cave. But finally the little Autobot nods his head.

"More Decepticons might be in the back of the cave," Mirage speculates. "What's our plan?"

"I'm for a direct attack on the poisons," Prowl says. "My incendiary missiles could wipe out everything in one shot."

"Sounds a little risky to me," Optimus Prime counters. "The four of us could overpower Ramjet and Starscream first. Then we could get rid of the poisons in a safer way."

Another tough decision! Which path is best?

To blow up the poisons, turn to page 9.
To tackle the two Decepticons, turn to page 30.

"Yikes!" Bumblebee thinks to himself. "I've got to get out of here!"

The brave mini-car steps on the gas. He shoots right between Laserbeak's powerful legs. Ahead, he can see the light coming from the entrance of the cave. Using every bit of his horsepower, he zooms toward it.

"Ouch!" the Autobot cries as Laserbeak's guns hit his rear fenders. Bumblebee zigzags back and forth to avoid the Decepticon's fire. But he gets hit by the laser cannons three more times.

Finally he escapes from the Poison Lab. He rushes out to join Optimus Prime and the others.

· ·

Turn to page 60.

Outside, Optimus Prime leads the way to a big pit just below headquarters.

"This will be the poison pit," he tells Grapple. "Remember, treat that tank as gently as a lilleth egg," says Optimus Prime, referring to the lovely glasslike birds of their home planet, Cybertron.

Grapple pushes his levers down and slowly lowers his load.

"Easy, easy," the Autobot leader cautions.

At last the tank lands at the bottom of the pit with a soft plop!

"There's your egg," Grapple says proudly, "ready to fry the Decepticons!"

Optimus Prime hurries down to open the tank's valves. The poisoned fuel flows out into the pit.

"Jazz!" Optimus Prime calls out.

"Right here," the cool sports car replies from his leader's side. "I'm warming up my flamethrower."

"The rest of you get inside. You should be safe from the fumes," Optimus Prime orders. "The Decepticons are in sight!"

Jazz looks at the western sky. Decepticon planes dot the horizon like a horde of insects.

"We have to wait until the last . . . possible . . . second," Optimus Prime tells Jazz.

. . . .

Turn to page 31.

On the rocky cliff outside Autobot headquarters, Sunstreaker directs the fighting robots to their battle stations.

"Take cover behind those boulders," he orders. "And don't fire until you see the purple of their Decepticon symbols!"

The Autobots fan out in a line of attack across the front of their headquarters. And not a second too soon!

A formation of Decepticon planes swoops down from the western sky. The sneaky Ramjet flies at the side of the mighty Megatron. They lead the evil Decepticons in the attack.

"NOW!" Sunstreaker yells as the Decepticons draw within firing range. Training the sights of his laser gun on Megatron's nose, the robot shoots a burst of ground-to-air rockets at the enemy leader.

Megatron hesitates in midair. Sunstreaker has stunned him. But not for long enough! With a scream of pain, he orders the Decepticons to fire!

Turn to page 17.

"We must find an antidote," says Optimus Prime. "In the meantime, Sparkplug, go get the emergency fuel. I hope we won't have to use it. I don't believe a small force can win this day!

"Our fate is in your hands, Perceptor," Optimus Prime tells the scientist as their human friend speeds off. "We can do nothing until you find the antidote to the poison that's blocking our ability to transform!"

Turn to page 66.

Before the Decepticons get off their first round of firepower, Warpath and Brawn attack. The macho Brawn tosses a boulder into the air at Ramjet. It clips his wing and sends him spinning to the ground. Warpath fires a barrage of acid shells at the Decepticons behind Megatron. Their formation splits apart in disarray.

For a few moments it seems that Sunstreaker's strategy will triumph. The enemy are buzzing in the sky like a swarm of confused flies.

Then Megatron strikes! His nuclear-charged fusion cannon shakes the earth. A bomb explodes right in the middle of the Autobots. Sunstreaker reels from the shock and falls in a heap.

Ratchet rushes from Autobot headquarters to put the pieces back together again. Seeing that the fighting Autobots are in trouble, Optimus Prime leads the others out into the battle.

"Make every shot count!" he cries, blasting Shockwave with his laser rifle.

Will the Autobot fuel last long enough to defeat the Decepticons?

Turn to page 34 to find out!

"I'm ready to fight!" Sunstreaker exclaims. "Let's go on the offensive."

A rumble of agreement swells up from the cured Autobots. Perceptor's antidote has given them all a case of battle fever.

"You forget one problem," Optimus Prime cuts in. "Half of us are almost out of fuel. An offensive would waste our valuable energy."

"Leave it to us," Sunstreaker says confidently. "We'll make those Decepticons turn tail and run."

"Or we could use our brains instead of our mouths," Prowl retaliates. "This could be our big chance to ambush those tin-plated tyrants! The Decepticons think we're all lying dead in here from their poison. We could play dead and trap them with their guard down."

. . . .

Do you have battle fever like Sunstreaker? To go on the offensive, turn to page 21.

Like the idea of playing dead and trapping the Decepticons? Sneak on to page 46.

18

Optimus Prime decides to turn the Decepticon poison against them. He surveys the Autobots still in working condition.

"Grapple," he says, "we need your strength and skill. You must transport this Decepticon poison outside."

Grapple shifts his powerful gears and moves to the huge silver tank. Optimus Prime secures steel cables around it; then he hooks them up to Grapple's crane.

"Stand back, Autobots," the construction vehicle orders.

"Wow!" Bumblebee shouts as Grapple grinds his gears and picks up the tank.

"Clear way," Optimus Prime bellows, and the Autobots instantly clear a path for Grapple to the door of headquarters.

Just then Red Alert zooms in, his sirens screaming.

"Ten minutes!" he shouts. "They'll be here in ten minutes!"

"Cool it, Red Alert," Grapple shouts, "or you'll get a real hot bath. I need room to pass!"

Red Alert shifts into reverse and screeches out of Grapple's way.

Turn to page 13.

The Autobots hurry from the cave as Ramjet and Starscream turn away. They pass Laserbeak at the entrance. Luckily, he's still in Decepticon Dreamland.

"Pleasant dreams, Laserfreak!" Bumblebee says.

Laughing over their victory, the Autobots wade through the polluted stream and begin their journey home. Optimus Prime carries the antidote in the cab of his truck. Prowl and Mirage follow him closely over the rugged terrain. Only Bumblebee trails behind, happily sniffing the fresh pine-scented air.

Two hours later Optimus Prime coasts into headquarters. But he isn't greeted by sounds of joy. Instead, his home lies as silent as a tomb.

"Prime!" Ratchet calls out. "You may be too late. Look at them!"

Wheezing Autobots are stretched out across the floor. From some, there is not even a flicker of life!

Turn to page 44.

Sunstreaker yells a battle cry: "Let's go for them!"

Warpath, Brawn, Bluestreak, and the other Auto-bots revived by Perceptor's antidote follow him outside. Optimus Prime turns to the remaining Autobots, who are nearly running on empty.

"Save your fuel," he warns. "We'll back up the others if they get into trouble."

"I don't like this," Prowl grumbles as he checks his fuel gauge. "I don't like it one bit!"

Turn to page 15.

Bumblebee reaches for the beaker and grabs it. In a flash, he transforms back into his mini-car shape to make a fast getaway. But wait! The snoring has stopped!

A second later the cruel voice of Laserbeak makes a chill run down Bumblebee's drive shaft.

"Stop!" the Decepticon commands. "Or I'll shoot!"

The little Autobot hesitates. What should he do?

. . . .

If you want Bumblebee to make a run for it, turn to page 12.

If you think he'd better do as the deadly Decepticon says, turn to page 68.

"Good thinking, Prowl," Optimus Prime says. "The Decepticons have sabotaged us. We must learn the secret of their poison and find out what else they have planned."

"Take me with you," Prowl requests. "This mission requires brains, not brawn!" he adds, pointing at Ironhide.

An angry grumble comes from old Ironhide, not famous for his brainpower.

"Prowl is right," the leader agrees. "Bumblebee, Mirage," he calls out. "We'll need you for espionage and intelligence gathering. The four of us will infiltrate the Decepticon hideout."

Ironhide rolls his headlights and growls as Prowl smirks at him. Just then Sparkplug pulls up in his truck. A metal gasoline drum sits on its bed.

"I got out the emergency fuel from the special storage area," he tells Optimus Prime. "After this is gone, Autobot headquarters will be completely dry."

"We'll make sure we use every gallon to foil the Decepticons," the Autobot leader declares.

Then he, Prowl, Mirage, and Bumblebee fuel up.

"Sparkplug," Optimus Prime adds, "you've already done so much for us, but somehow you've got to find us a new supply of fuel as soon as possible! Here we go! With luck, we will return with a cure for the Decepticon poison!"

....

Turn to page 36.

"We'll go in together," Optimus Prime announces. "I'll lead the way."

The four Autobots move out of their cover behind the huge redwood. Quietly they creep across the brown, scorched earth. As they near the mouth of the cave, Prowl whispers a warning.

"We must be careful," he says. "This is a Decepticon stronghold. They wouldn't leave it unguarded."

Truer words were never spoken, for just then Laserbeak, the Decepticon interrogator, steps out of the dark cave.

"Uninvited guests, I see," he snarls, unshielding his laser guns.

But Optimus Prime is the fastest draw in the Northwest! He whips out *his* laser gun and silently blasts away at Laserbeak. The Decepticon crumbles to the ground, his circuits shot.

"Hurry," the Autobot leader orders. "Inside."

Turn to page 3.

Mirage reaches the dark shadows of the boulders. Instantly he regains his true identity.

"Nice timing," Optimus Prime congratulates him. "A little risky, but nice."

"I overheard Ramjet and Starscream talking," Mirage tells his leader. "If I heard them correctly, they're planning something truly unspeakable!"

Turn to page 69.

"Autobots, *transform!*" Optimus Prime commands.

Whoops of joy echo through headquarters. The transforming mechanisms are in working order again. The robots slap each other on the back and flex their muscles.

"I want revenge!" Sunstreaker yells. "Let's go get the Decepticons!"

"You're right, Sunstreaker," Optimus Prime answers. "We must battle our enemy. But our cause is not revenge. We must save our human friends from the Decepticon poison!"

Turn to page 56.

Well, somebody's got to save the humans. It may as well be Powerglide. He zooms into the air.

The airborne Autobot looks down at his comrades. They're watching him with upturned headlights.

"Here I go!" he yells.

Powerglide swoops and turns and spins through the sky. The Decepticon planes rev their engines, trying to figure out which way he'll go next. Soon the air around the Autobot explodes with enemy fire.

"Ha!" the clever show-off taunts as he dodges Ramjet's cluster bombs.

"Ha ha!" he cries as he sidesteps Ravage's proton bombs. They splatter into the water below.

Below him, Powerglide spies Frenzy. He drops a concussion bomb on the unsuspecting Decepticon.

Wham! Frenzy goes into a tailspin. He is headed for a nosedive into the water.

Seconds later, disaster!

Turn to page 45.

The Autobots prepare their weapons for a sneak attack on the two Decepticons. With Optimus Prime in the lead, they steal across the cave to within close range.

"Drop your guns!" the Autobot leader commands.

Ramjet and Starscream whirl around in amazement.

"Never!" Starscream screams.

The violent Decepticon goes on the attack. He shoots a spray of null-rays at the Autobots.

"Laserbeak, help!" Ramjet yells as Optimus Prime grabs his weapons.

Meanwhile, Prowl and Mirage wrestle Starscream to the floor of the cave. Bumblebee stuffs a rock into his mouth to keep him quiet.

"Wow, these guys aren't so tough when they're grounded," Mirage says. "They're murder only in the air."

The Autobots securely lash cables of indestructible steel around their enemies.

"Now watch," Optimus Prime tells them, "as your evil work is destroyed!"

. . . .

Turn to page 4.

The roar of the Decepticon jets is louder now. In seconds they will be right over the poison pit!

"Now!" the Autobot leader shouts.

Jazz activates his flamethrower. A ribbon of fire shoots out of it. With a fiery whoosh, it hits the poison pit. The burning gas leaps into the sky like a huge, orange hot-air balloon.

"Wow!" Jazz exclaims, impressed by his own work.

"Run for it!" Optimus Prime yells, grabbing Jazz to make a hasty retreat. Seconds later, they dive inside headquarters.

Up in the air, Ramjet and Starscream are in the middle of their attack dives as the poison gas ignites. They turn their noses upward and try to swoop above the pit. But it's too late!

The Decepticons choke and sputter. Ramjet crashes into the hillside with a bad dose of his own medicine. Starscream makes an emergency landing too close to the fiery pit. His metal parts begin to melt into a putrid puddle.

It looks like the Decepticons are done for. But wait! There, on the horizon, are two of the most dreaded Decepticons, Frenzy and Laserbeak!

Turn to page 58.

"Transform," Optimus Prime commands. "We've got to get across that stream and investigate that Decepticon lab—if that's what it is."

The Autobots step into the gooey orange water and wade through the sludge.

"Ow-w-w-w!" Bumblebee yells. The acid in the water is biting into his metal feet.

At last the four reach the safety of another huge redwood. The Decepticon lab stands in front of them, reeking with the smell of poison.

"Now what?" Mirage asks.

The Autobots are in a dangerous spot. Should they enter the lab together? After all, there's safety in numbers. Or should Bumblebee, the espionage expert, go in alone? It's your decision!

To send in all four, turn to page 25.
To send in Bumblebee alone, turn to page 39.

"Then I'm afraid you have only two choices," the scientist explains. "First, you can try the antidote. It has not been tested, and I cannot be sure it will work. Also, I can't guarantee there will be no side effects for the Autobots. On the other hand, this is not a very complex poison, and I do believe there is at least a fighting chance that the antidote will work."

"What's the other choice?" asks Optimus Prime gravely.

"I believe that, when burned, this fuel will give off poisonous fumes," says Perceptor. "Perhaps we could set fire to the fuel and use it against the Decepticons."

"That's an interesting plan, Perceptor." Optimus Prime considers the idea of turning the poison against the poisoners.

"Yes," agrees Perceptor. "But it is also a dangerous plan. The fire could easily get out of control, and I am not sure that *we* will be safe from the poison!"

This is a terrible decision to make. The poisoned Autobots are growing weaker and weaker. The Decepticons are getting closer and closer.

There's no time to waste! What should Optimus Prime do?

. . . .

Give the antidote? Turn to page 41.
Use the fuel as a defense? Turn to page 19.

33

The battle rages on. Autobots and Decepticons trade bombs and bullets. Then, suddenly, Optimus Prime feels a dreaded weakening in his fuel lines.

"Below empty!" he gasps, checking his gauge. Prowl, Grapple, and the other Autobots low on gas begin to sputter to a stop around him.

"Retreat!" their leader orders in a choking voice. "Back into headquarters!"

Grapple manages enough strength to pull several of the injured with him into the safety of headquarters. Sunstreaker is the last in, taking heavy fire from the gleeful Decepticons. As the yellow-and-orange robot collapses in an exhausted heap, Red Alert peers through his security window.

"They're retreating!" he announces. "We must have scored more hits than we thought."

"We have survived," Optimus Prime declares, "but the fight is far from over. We must fight until the universe is free of *all* the Decepticon poison!"

THE END

34

The four Autobots set off on their mission. They travel west, in the direction of Ramjet's getaway path.

Optimus Prime takes the lead. His huge tractor-trailer wheels cut a path for the smaller cars to follow.

"Whew!" Bumblebee gasps. "This is rough going."

The yellow mini-car trails behind the others. Their route twists through the dense pine trees surrounding Autobot headquarters.

A high mountain looms ahead. Optimus Prime shifts into a lower gear as he begins the climb.

"Follow me!" he roars, grinding up the steep incline.

Halfway to the top the four vehicles stop for a rest.

"We've gone a hundred miles," Mirage pants, trying to cool his engine. "And no Decepticons are in sight!"

The Autobots search the countryside around them. They see green fir trees swaying in the wind. Winding rivers rush westward to the Pacific. The rugged terrain seems untouched by civilization.

"Keep climbing," Optimus Prime orders. "Who knows what's on the other side of this mountain."

At last they reach the peak. Gazing down into the valley below, Bumblebee lets out a low whistle.

"Creepy!" he mutters.

Turn to page 10.

"*Halt!*" the Autobot leader shouts.

Powerglide quickly throws his engines into reverse. The Autobot screeches to a halt on the flat plain.

"Your idea was brave . . . but foolish," Optimus Prime says as he approaches Powerglide. "You could not take on all those planes alone!"

"But how are we going to stop them?" Powerglide asks.

"They're headed in our direction," Bluestreak calls out. "Should we get ready to fight?"

"We only have one choice," Optimus Prime announces. "We must divert them away from the water. Out here we are helpless against an enemy attack. But if we can move into the forest, we will have some cover."

Turn to page 55.

"Halt!" the Autobot leader commands.

The caravan of cars and trucks comes to a stop at the edge of the reservoir.

"We're like sitting ducks here," Prowl says. "The Decepticons will fill us with birdshot."

"Our position is vulnerable," Optimus Prime agrees grimly.

Meanwhile, Powerglide is busy adjusting his mechanical parts. One of the few Autobots who can fly, he loves to show off. And this seems like the perfect chance!

"I'll give them a goose chase," he calls out. Powerglide thrusts his engines forward and taxis across the plain.

"No!" Optimus Prime booms.

But the brave, flying Autobot speeds away. Is this a suicide mission? You have the power to stop him. *Or* you can let him go.

The decision is yours!

To send Powerglide into the air, turn to page 29.
To cut his engines, turn to page 37.

"Me—gulp—go in there alone?" Bumblebee murmurs. "Okay, but I wish I had a gas mask—not for the poison, but for the stench of the Decepticons!"

The other Autobots wish Bumblebee good luck. Then the brave mini-car sneaks into the cave. His excellent vision immediately adjusts to the dim light. To his horror, he sees a figure leaning against the wall. It's Laserbeak, the cruel Decepticon interrogator!

Bumblebee freezes. Then, slowly, a grin spreads across his face. Laserbeak is asleep! His snore vibrates through the cave like a chain saw. The little Autobot sneaks by the cruel Decepticon, penetrating the depths of the lab.

Bumblebee moves from one dark recess to another. At last he sees rows of beakers bubbling away on blue flames. The espionage expert narrows his eyes to read the labels written in a secret Decepticon code.

"Aha!" he whispers as he deciphers one of the labels. "Autobot Poison Antidote!"

Turn to page 23.

Ramjet, Skywarp, and a rewired Laserbeak are pushing something from the depths of the cave. Their grunts and groans echo up the mountainside.

"Black tanks," Brawn mutters. "They look like coffins!"

"That's what they'll be for the humans," Optimus Prime says grimly, "if we don't stop the Decepticons here!"

The Decepticons push ten of the tanks in front of the Poison Lab. Each is marked with the Decepticon symbol.

Turn to page 70.

Optimus Prime decides to try the untested antidote. He can't bear to hear the moans and groans of his fallen troops.

Perceptor clutches the beaker full of antidote. He quickly thinks about the chemicals he has combined. Did he mix the right compounds? Did he pour in the right amounts? Will this stuff work??

With Optimus Prime beside him, the scientist walks up to the weakened Autobots.

"It's in your hands now, Perceptor," his leader tells him. "The antidote is our only hope!"

With trembling hands, Perceptor begins to measure out the antidote. One milliliter or two—that is the question. One milliliter is a safe amount, but will it be strong enough against Decepticon poison? Two milliliters would take care of the poison, but would it be too powerful for the cars to handle?

Time is running out. Perceptor must decide now!

. . . .

If you think the one-milliliter dose is enough, turn to page 62.

If you think the two-milliliter dose is a better shot, turn to page 50.

"Start your engines," Optimus Prime orders the Autobots, "and *transform*!"

As the antidote courses through their fuel lines, the injured Autobots effortlessly change into their robot forms.

Cheering erupts in headquarters. Sunstreaker and Brawn hoist Perceptor onto their shoulders like a hero. But seconds later, disaster strikes!

Sunstreaker and Brawn crumble to the ground, dropping Perceptor as they fall. Their arms and legs snap off their bodies. Perceptor stares in horror at the other Autobots he treated. Their joints are breaking off too. Parts of the Autobots hit the floor with sickening crashes.

"A major miscalculation!" the scientist murmurs as Ratchet desperately tries to put the Autobots back together.

Just then the roar of Deception engines fills the air.

Perceptor's miscalculation has left the Autobots real shorthanded (and shortlegged). The Decepticons will make short work of them now.

THE END

"Ratchet!" Optimus Prime calls out. "I need your help."

The spry mechanic goes to work with the Autobot leader. They pour a dose of medicine into each gasping gas tank.

Then Optimus Prime kneels in the midst of his injured friends. He addresses them in a soft but powerful voice.

"Get well," he urges them. "You must try. Start your engines. Let the antidote flow through your gas lines."

A weak sputter comes from Sunstreaker. He tries to turn his engine over. It fails. The brave Autobot tries again. And again. At last the soft purr of his motor fills the air!

The worried face of Optimus Prime breaks into a wide smile. The other Autobots are coming to life too. Soon headquarters is filled with the roar of racing engines!

Turn to page 27.

Frenzy crashes into the crystal-clear reservoir. The impact explodes two tanks of Decepticon poison which he was carrying under his wings. Then a putrid orange stain spreads across the water.

On the ground, Optimus Prime watches in horror. The Autobots' mission has failed. The Decepticons will control the humans. Unless . . . unless another antidote can be found.

The only real antidote now is to close the book . . . and find a happier fate to follow!

THE END

"Cool your jets, Sunstreaker," Optimus Prime commands. "The Decepticons played a dirty trick on us, and this is our chance to get back at them. We're going to lure them in here by playing dead. What will our strategy be, Prowl?"

The logical Autobot runs several plans through his brain circuits. Then he explains his best idea to Optimus Prime.

"Transform into vehicles," the leader orders. "Then shut down your engines . . . and wait!"

Within seconds the Autobot headquarters is as silent as a tomb. Even when the roar of Decepticon planes grows louder and louder, the brave cars and trucks do not flinch a gear.

Soon the powerful voice of Megatron echoes through the vast room. The cruel Decepticon leader, transformed into his giant robot shape, enters Autobot headquarters, followed by his evil comrades.

"The poison has worked," Megatron sneers. "The Autobots are dead!"

What happens now? To find out, turn to page 51.

The poisons explode into sheets of flame. "Oh, no!" Bumblebee screams. "*Fire!*"

The Autobots feel their circuits overheating. They slump to the floor of the cave, unconscious. And as the beaker of antidote falls from Mirage's hand, it shatters into millions of tiny pieces!

An hour later the fallen Autobots begin to stir. Their eyes flicker open . . . and they stare at the evil smile of . . . Megatron!

"Your plan *back*fired," the Decepticon leader laughs at them. "You are now our prisoners. And your friends at headquarters will never, never get well again. As for the humans, we will conquer them next!"

Prowl covers his face in shame. His strategy was a disaster. He wishes you had picked a different path! And so do you, since you and the rest of humankind must now drink from the poisoned, bitter cup of failure! Bottoms up!

THE END

The first blast of firepower is earthshaking! Ironhide sprays the Poison Lab with superheated lead. Twin Twist shoots out 100-pound TNT shells from his cannon rifle. Brawn demolishes the poison tanks with a single blow of his powerful fist. Hound fires his turret gun at the startled Decepticons.

Optimus Prime aims his heavy artillery at the cracks in the top of the cave. *Boom!* Rocks and dust explode in the air.

"Listen!" Prowl tells the cheering Autobots.

A deep rumble grows louder and louder inside the Poison Lab.

"The lab!" Mirage shouts. "It's caving in!"

There is a final roar of falling rock. Then the Decepticon hideout collapses under a cloud of poisonous yellow dust.

"Nice show!" Bumblebee yells.

"Too bad the Decepticons missed the end," Sunstreaker adds. "It was the best part!"

THE END

Perceptor stares at the marks on his measuring vial as he pours the antidote. *One milliliter . . . one and a half . . . two milliliters!* The scientist unscrews Sunstreaker's gas cap and pours in the amber liquid.

"I don't like being a guinea pig," the sports car sputters. "I hope this stuff works!"

Ratchet helps the scientist give the other Autobots their dose of medicine. Just as Perceptor pours the last drop of antidote into Bluestreak's tank, Red Alert rushes in with an announcement.

"Ramjet is in the lead with all the Decepticons behind him! It's an all-out attack!" he screams.

Quick! Turn to page 43.

Ramjet, Shockwave, Laserbeak, and more smirking Decepticons crowd around Megatron.

"Look at this pile of tin," Ramjet snickers, kicking Sunstreaker's sleek fender.

Megatron joins in the Decepticon laughter. Then he commands, "Drop your weapons and dispose of this garbage. We'll push them over the cliff outside."

Optimus Prime's headlights begin to glow brighter and brighter as the Decepticons disarm themselves. Then, with a mighty roar, he issues a command.

"Autobots, *transform!*"

In front of the Decepticons' amazed eyes, the Autobots rise from the dead like ghosts!

There is a gleam of panic in Megatron's eyes.

"Run!" he screams, his voice unusually high.

"Fire!" Optimus Prime shouts.

The battle begins. And, as you might guess, the Decepticons don't stand a ghost of a chance!

THE END

Optimus Prime calls forth his big guns for an all-out attack! "Brawn, Twin Twist, Ironhide, Hound!"

The mighty Autobots line up beside their leader.

"Here come the fireworks!" Bumblebee shouts with excitement.

"Ready!" the Autobot leader announces. "Aim! Fire!"

Turn to page 49.

Laserbeak blasts away at the little Autobot. But Bumblebee clamps shut his hood and doesn't answer a single question. All the brave mini-car can do is think of his hero—Optimus Prime.

Don't you feel just awful? You made a bad choice! But don't worry. Bumblebee will survive in another ending.

As for Laserbeak, why doesn't he pick on somebody his own size?

THE END

The Autobots head north away from the reservoir toward a stand of pine trees five miles away. If they can make it there, the forest will give them cover from an air attack.

But the sound of the Decepticon engines grows louder and louder. The Autobot leader sees that a rear attack is imminent.

"Stand your ground," he commands, "and *transform!*"

The Autobots flash into their warrior shapes and whip out their weapons.

"Fire!" Optimus Prime orders.

A barrage of bullets smashes into the oncoming Decepticon planes. Some bounce off the tough, armored skins of the enemy jets. But others find their targets, splintering the engines of Starscream, Thundercracker, and Soundwave. The three Decepticons spin dizzily to the ground. They dig their own charred graves in the brown earth.

. . . .

Turn to page 71.

At that moment Sparkplug drives into headquarters at the wheel of a huge gas tanker. He brakes to a stop and climbs out of the cab.

"I did manage to come up with some fuel, Chief," he says. "Get in line and I'll fill you up for the fight."

The Autobots jostle each other for a place in the fuel line. Meanwhile, Optimus Prime calls a strategy session with a few of his top warriors.

They huddle together, trying to figure out how to stop the Decepticons from poisoning the humans' drinking water!

Turn to page 59.

The noble leader of the Autobots takes aim at the two enemy planes carrying the black, coffinlike tanks of poison. His sophisticated brain center calculates their rate of speed and projected flight pattern. Then he takes a firm grip on the laser guns in each of his hands.

KERPLOW!

KERPLOW!

Optimus Prime picks off both Decepticon bombers in midair. They spiral to the earth, trailing black poison clouds after them.

Megatron roars with fury and launches another offensive against the Autobots. The warring robots trade one crushing blow after another.

The battle rages on until nightfall. At last Megatron and his warriors retreat into the darkened sky.

A band of stricken Autobots gasps in exhaustion on the scorched plain. Ratchet goes to work, trying to put their pieces back together again.

The forces of good have survived. The Autobot mission has been accomplished. The humans never find out how close they came to being Decepticon slaves. You're the only one who knows—and you'll keep the secret right up to . . .

THE END

The two battle-crazy Decepticons dive through the poison cloud to charge Autobot headquarters. They drop bombs that make the Autobots reel inside their home.

But the enemy planes have lingered too long in the cloud of poison fumes. Their engines hesitate . . . then sputter . . . then choke. Frenzy and Laserbeak go into wild tailspins. The rest of the Decepticon attack force sees them, turns tail, and runs back home.

Inside headquarters, the Autobots erupt into victory cheers.

"When a big battle comes," Bumblebee shouts, "the Decepticons always choke!"

"Rats! Am I too late for the action?" Sunstreaker yells, rushing up to Optimus Prime.

"But . . . you're supposed to be sick!" the leader says in amazement. "You were poisoned!"

. . . .

How is this possible? Turn to page 63 to find out!

"We have two choices for our battle site," the leader explains to his comrades. "The first is the Decepticon Poison Lab. The second is the humans' water reservoir."

The Autobots argue the pros and cons of the two sites. The route to the Poison Lab is familiar to them. They may be able to sneak up on the Decepticons there.

But there is a troubling possibility. The Decepticons may have already left the lab with the poison. It might be best to rush to the reservoir first, even though it is a greater distance away. The trouble is . . . a battle on the flat plain around the reservoir could be very dangerous.

Which strategy do you think is best?
Fight at the Poison Lab? Turn to page 7.
Head for the reservoir? Turn to page 67.

"Well done, Bumblebee!" the Autobot leader exclaims. He takes the beaker of antidote from the trembling mini-car.

"Laserbeak's behind me!" Bumblebee warns the others. "We gotta get away. *Fast!*"

Optimus Prime hoists the little guy on his broad shoulders. Then the four Autobots make their escape from the Valley of Poison.

Later, at headquarters, the ailing Autobots are restored to health. Sparkplug arrives with a new supply of fuel. Everyone drinks a high-octane toast to the hero of the day—Bumblebee, who stole the antidote right from under the Decepticons' noses! No, wait! Make that right from under their beaks—their Laserbeaks!

THE END

Mirage formulates his strategy.

"This is my plan," the clever Autobot whispers to Optimus Prime. "I'll use my electro-disrupter to cast an illusion so that I look just like Laserbeak. Even if the other Decepticons see me, they'll never suspect I'm an Autobot."

"Don't forget one thing," Prowl warns. "Your illusions last only six minutes. You have to work fast!"

The silver-and-blue Autobot smiles confidently. Then, with a surge of energy, he changes his image. Magically, he reappears as the evil Laserbeak!

The others watch Mirage stride toward the Poison Lab. He reaches out his hand to grab the antidote. As his fingers close around the beaker, Ramjet and Starscream enter the room.

They stare at the illusion of Laserbeak. Mirage stares back at them through Laserbeak's eyes. Finally, Ramjet and Starscream turn away.

"He's got only thirty seconds left!" Bumblebee murmurs.

Mirage begins to stroll calmly back to the Autobots' hiding place.

"Three seconds left!" Bumblebee whispers.

Turn to page 26.

"Better safe than sorry," Perceptor says as he pours a one-milliliter dose of antidote into Sunstreaker's tank.

Perceptor's hands shake as he gives all the injured Autobots a dose of the antidote. Trying an untested chemical offends his rational, careful mind. But these are desperate times!

Sunstreaker and the others begin to rev up their engines. The antidote shoots through their fuel lines, cancelling out the Decepticon poison.

Within seconds the vehicles have transformed into mighty robots.

"I feel like a new Autobot!" Sunstreaker roars, flexing his iron forearms.

Optimus Prime strides into the midst of his restored warriors.

"There's no time for celebration, Autobots," he says. "The Decepticons are coming!"

Turn to page 18.

"Me . . . sick?" Sunstreaker asks, flexing his orange muscles. "I'm the guinea pig. Perceptor poured some of his antidote into my gas tank, and now I feel like decking some Decepticons."

"Save your energy," Optimus Prime tells him with a smile, "at least until we get a new supply of fuel!"

THE END

"Windcharger, you take the lead," Optimus Prime commands.

The Autobots ready their weapons. The tanks of poison sit unprotected in front of the cave. Skywarp, Laserbeak, and Ramjet are sprawled on the ground, taking a rest.

"Let the attack begin!" Optimus Prime orders.

Windcharger, the fastest Autobot over short distances, zooms forward. In a blur of speed, he unleashes his powerful magnetic gun. Aiming it at the cave, he casts a magnetic field over the tanks.

Like magic, the huge containers begin to move. The Decepticons watch with amazed eyes as the poison tanks mysteriously rise off the ground.

"Your turn, Prowl," Optimus Prime says with a grin.

Prowl steps forward and takes aim. He riddles the tanks with highly corrosive acid pellets. The poison spurts out of a thousand holes!

"Finish off the job, Jazz," the Autobot leader commands.

"I can't wait for this part," Bumblebee giggles.

Turn to page 72.

Without saying a word, Perceptor rushes off to his laboratory with a beaker of poisoned fuel. He knows what he must do.

"I feel sick," Sunstreaker moans weakly.

"Me too," Warpath adds, groaning with pain.

Optimus Prime tries to cheer up the injured Autobots. But soon a bleak silence falls over Autobot headquarters. Perceptor works feverishly in his laboratory, knowing time is not on his side!

The stillness is broken when Red Alert bursts into the room again.

"My sensors have picked up a Decepticon attack force," he tells Optimus Prime. "They're still a distance away, but they're moving fast!"

As Red Alert hurries back to his post, Optimus Prime strides over to Perceptor's laboratory. The scientist is hunched over several beakers of bubbling liquid.

"Time has run out," Optimus Prime announces. "What are your results?"

"I have an antidote," the scientist exclaims, "but I need more time to test it."

"There is no time," Optimus declares. "We must act now or it will be too late!"

Turn to page 33.

"The Decepticons' target," Optimus Prime says, pointing to a map, "is the humans' water reservoir. If the water supply is poisoned, our earth friends will be nothing but Decepticon slaves! We must go there now and foil their evil plot!

"Brawn, you will take the lead there," the leader commands. "Now, let's roll!"

The macho Brawn guns his engine, proud to lead the troops. He roars out of headquarters. A caravan of angry Autobots follows.

The route to the reservoir is challenging. The vehicles screech around winding mountain roads. They ford rushing streams. They plow through volcanic ash. At last the Autobots race across the flat, unprotected plain around the humans' water supply.

"Look, up in the sky!" Red Alert calls out above the roar of engines.

The Autobots direct their headlights over the reservoir. The air is filled with a black horde of Decepticon planes!

Turn to page 38.

Trembling with fear, Bumblebee slams on his emergency brake. Laserbeak strides over to him with giant steps and grabs the antidote.

"So . . . . you want to save your sick friends, eh?" he snarls. "When I get finished with you, you'll wish you'd never tried."

Bumblebee cowers in the shadow of the huge Decepticon. What will he do now? One thing is sure. He'll never betray his fellow Autobots!

Laserbeak snaps out his two laser cannons.

"Tools of my trade," he snickers. "They make my prisoners talk every time."

"Not me!" Bumblebee says defiantly.

This is terrible! Turn to page 54.

The Autobots creep around to the other side of the cave to eavesdrop. The two Decepticons are gloating over their latest use of the Poison Lab. They go over their plot within earshot of the horrified Autobots.

"Did you hear that?" Prowl asks angrily after the two Decepticons move to the lab.

"They want to poison the humans' water reservoir. They have a secret chemical that will make our earth friends their slaves!" Optimus Prime mutters.

"What . . . what are we going to do about it?" Bumblebee asks. "We'd better take this antidote back to headquarters. Then all the Autobots can help foil their plan."

"That might take too much time," Prowl considers. "We may have to act immediately!"

Now the lives of humans are at stake too. That means you! What is your next move?

To send the Autobots back to headquarters, and return with a full Autobot army, turn to page 5.

To take action now, turn to page 11.

69

"The poison," Mirage whispers. "It must be in those tanks. They're waiting for it to be picked up."

"Let's give them a surprise party first," Sunstreaker exclaims.

The Autobots are ready for action! Everybody has a plan and a strategy to offer.

"Let me take the lead," Windcharger tells Optimus Prime. "I'm the fastest. I'll zip in there and use my magnetic force field on the poison tanks. Then the rest of you can come in and do the 'cleanup.'"

Ironhide disagrees. "Don't get fancy," he says gruffly. "Let's just get in there and attack. Full force. Nice and simple!" Windcharger's plan has more style, but Ironhide's has more force. Which do you think will carry the day?

If you want to let Windcharger take the lead, turn to page 64.

If you want to try an all-out attack, turn to page 53.

With a roar of angry engines, the other Decepticons regroup for an attack. Mighty Megatron is in the lead.

At his command, a furious attack explodes around the Autobots. With shattering robot parts flying through the air, Bluestreak, Hound, and Mirage bite the dust.

Optimus Prime surveys the wreckage and grits his teeth. He must destroy the planes carrying the poison. *But will the Autobots be destroyed first?*

Turn to page 57.

Jazz whips out his flamethrower and shoots a spray of fire at the poison. The tanks explode in an orange cloud of flames.

"Autobots!" Laserbeak screams.

The three Decepticons try to get off a round of fire, but the heat is too intense for them. They scurry back into the darkness of the lab.

"Warpath," Optimus says, "the last shot is yours. Aim for the cave entrance with your sonic gun."

The sharpshooting warrior trains his sights on the distant entrance. He fires!

Seconds later the air is filled with the sound of shattering glass. Warpath's sonic boom destroys every beaker in the Decepticon Poison Lab!

With cheers of victory, the Autobots return to headquarters, happy that the Decepticons' plans have been completely shattered!

THE END